DARE *to be* DIFFERENT

A Celebration of Freedom in Association with Amnesty International

BLOOMSBURY CHILDREN'S BOOKS

AMNESTY INTERNATIONAL
UNITED KINGDOM

CONTENTS

INTRODUCTION

Amnesty International was launched in 1961 by a British lawyer, Peter Benenson, after he read about two Portuguese students who had been imprisoned for raising their glasses in a toast to freedom. He wrote a newspaper article called 'The Forgotten Prisoners' which brought in more than 1,000 offers of support for an international campaign to support human rights. Within 12 months the young organisation was making representations on behalf of prisoners around the world.

From its simple launch Amnesty International has become the world's largest international voluntary organisation dealing with human rights. Amnesty has more than one million members and supporters in over 170 countries and territories, who work to prevent some of the gravest violations by governments of people's fundamental human rights.

The organisation is independent of any government, political ideology, economic interest or religion. Amnesty International has a mandate which helps the organisation both define and limit its work and focus its energies, and its mandate is based on the Universal Declaration of Human Rights issued in 1948.

AMNESTY INTERNATIONAL
WORKS PRIMARILY

● to seek the release of prisoners of conscience — those imprisoned solely for their political, religious or other conscientiously held beliefs, or their ethnic origin, sex, colour, language, national or social status, and who have not used or advocated the use of violence.

● to work for fair and prompt trials for all political prisoners to campaign to abolish the death penalty, torture, and other cruel, inhuman or degrading treatment or punishment of all prisoners.

● to end extrajudicial executions and 'disappearances'.

ILLUSTRATION BY DAWN APPERLEY

During most of its history, Amnesty's campaigning has focused on prisoners, but the movement has responded to changing patterns of human rights violations in the world. Increasingly Amnesty International has taken action on behalf of people who are not prisoners. It does this in three main ways:

● by working against abuses by opposition groups: hostage taking; torture and killings of prisoners; and other arbitrary killings.

● by working for asylum seekers who are at risk of being returned to a country where they might be held as prisoners of conscience, 'disappear' or suffer torture or execution.

● by working for people who, because the non-violent expression of their beliefs, or by reason of their ethnic origin, sex, colour or language, are forcibly exiled from their country.

Through educational programmes and campaigns, Amnesty International works to promote all the human rights enshrined in The Universal Declaration of Human Rights and other international standards, and for human rights treaties to be ratified.

In this collection of writings, the contributors show that the principles of Amnesty International — principles of justice, equality and freedom — are principles that apply to us all and that through recognising these principles in our daily lives, as well as in the political arena, we can make a difference to the world. The writing in this book shows us that we can change the world for the better. It reminds us that our faith and beliefs can help us overcome apparently insurmountable problems. It also shows us that time and change can allow us to move on and enjoy an improved society. It tells us to believe in our dreams and, with firm action, make them come true. And most importantly, just like Amnesty International, the stories and poems celebrate the will and action of individuals to force and create positive change.

In this wonderful collection of stories and poems, classical and modern, and through the beautiful art, the beliefs and actions of Amnesty International are given a wonderful relevance that will speak to us all.

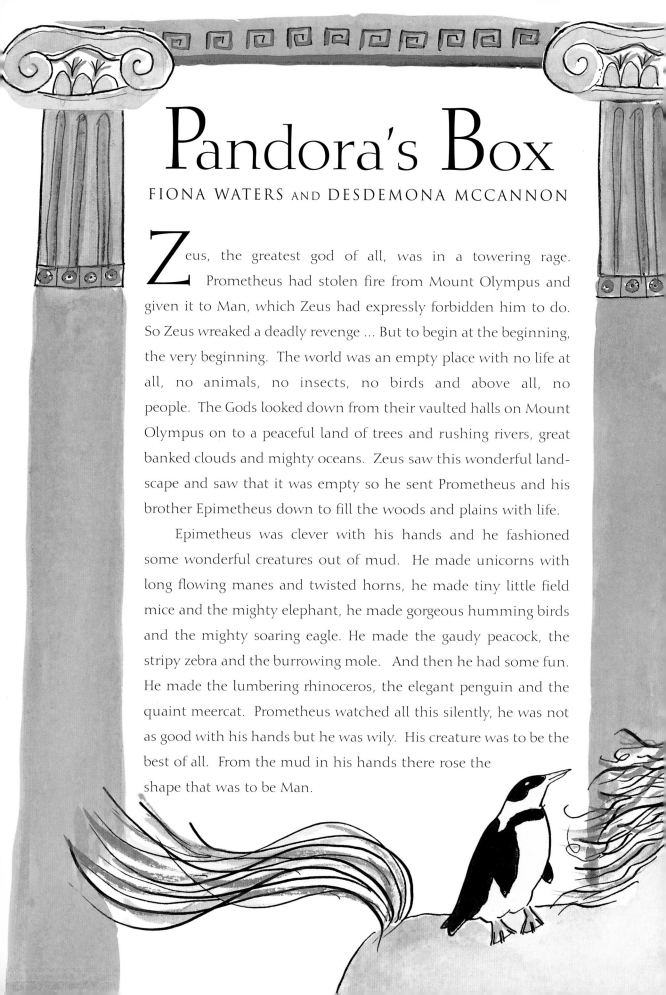

Pandora's Box

FIONA WATERS AND DESDEMONA MCCANNON

Zeus, the greatest god of all, was in a towering rage. Prometheus had stolen fire from Mount Olympus and given it to Man, which Zeus had expressly forbidden him to do. So Zeus wreaked a deadly revenge ... But to begin at the beginning, the very beginning. The world was an empty place with no life at all, no animals, no insects, no birds and above all, no people. The Gods looked down from their vaulted halls on Mount Olympus on to a peaceful land of trees and rushing rivers, great banked clouds and mighty oceans. Zeus saw this wonderful landscape and saw that it was empty so he sent Prometheus and his brother Epimetheus down to fill the woods and plains with life.

Epimetheus was clever with his hands and he fashioned some wonderful creatures out of mud. He made unicorns with long flowing manes and twisted horns, he made tiny little field mice and the mighty elephant, he made gorgeous humming birds and the mighty soaring eagle. He made the gaudy peacock, the stripy zebra and the burrowing mole. And then he had some fun. He made the lumbering rhinoceros, the elegant penguin and the quaint meercat. Prometheus watched all this silently, he was not as good with his hands but he was wily. His creature was to be the best of all. From the mud in his hands there rose the shape that was to be Man.

He was a poor creature this first man. Naked and cold and hungry, he would not survive long. So Prometheus asked Zeus to protect his creation by giving him fire to warm him through the long nights, to cook his food and to make pots to store water in. Zeus absolutely refused for he was afraid that this race of men might one day rise to challenge the power of the Gods. Prometheus was a Titan, one of the oldest of the Gods, and he was not pleased to be so thwarted by Zeus. He went at dead of night and stole a burning ember from the eternal fires at Olympus and bore it away to earth where he showed Man how to keep this fire alight. Of course it was not long before Zeus saw a glow of red on the earth and a wisp of smoke spiralling upwards, and he realised Prometheus had defied him. His revenge was swift and terrible. He chained Prometheus to a rock on a remote mountainside and sent an eagle to peck at his body every day. Gods never die so Prometheus had to endure this torture into eternity.

But Zeus did not stop there. He still felt threatened by this creature Man so he devised what at first looked like a reward. With the help of the other Gods, he created Woman. Aphrodite gave her beauty, Athene taught her the homely crafts of cooking and sewing. Hermes gave her guile and a silver tongue and Apollo taught her to play the lyre. And when she stood before him, Zeus looked and smiled and was well pleased. He called her Pandora. And then he sent for Epimetheus.

Epimetheus, you will remember, was a wonderful craftsman but he lacked his brother's quick wits so he was unsuspecting when Zeus gave him the beautiful Pandora for his bride. And he was even more unsuspecting when Zeus gave Pandora a great wooden box, closed with bands of steel and chains and many great padlocks as a wedding gift. Zeus commanded Pandora to keep the box always by her side but never, ever to open it under any circumstances. Pandora thought the box must be full of gold and jewels, Epimetheus never gave it another thought.

For a while all was well. Epimetheus was a kind and good man and he was well pleased with his beautiful new wife. She was vain and silly, but happy as long as Epimetheus was spoiling her and giving her everything she could possibly want. But the box preyed on her mind. What was the point of a present she could never open? Was it full of gold or fine cloth or silver caskets stuffed with rare jewels? Perhaps she could just have one little peep inside? But whenever she mentioned it, Epimetheus grew angry and told her sharply that she must never ever open it for Zeus' wrath would be great. Diverted for a while, she laughed and danced and sang her way through the days.

But still the box sat there, ever present, never revealing its secrets. The temptation just grew and grew until it occupied her every waking thought and indeed her dreams. Her curiosity grew to an obsession and she knew she would know no peace until the box was opened. She found herself standing by the box and then her fingers were on the steel bands and then her hands loosened the chains. And then she lifted the lid.

There was the sound of a mighty rushing wind and the room grew dark and icy cold. Out of the box flew all manner of evil. Disease, Pain, Cruelty, War, Poverty filled the room. And still the tide flowed. Old Age, Hate, Jealousy, Vice and Despair. Last of all came the most terrible, Death. They all stalked out into the wide world, leaving behind a terrified, sobbing Pandora. Now she knew why Zeus had been so insistent that the box remain closed. Now she knew she had lost her husband's love for ever. She alone was responsible for spoiling the paradise that was the Earth. And she flung herself across the box in a desperate attempt to shut the lid, but it was far, far too late. Zeus would have his revenge. The Gods would never again be threatened by Man.

Suddenly from within the box there came a faint tremor, a gentle rustle. Pandora looked down into its depth and it seemed the darkness eased a little as a tiny shaft of light glanced upwards. One last thing lay at the very bottom of the box. With trembling fingers Pandora eased the lid back fully, and with a sudden sweet breath out came Hope. It spread around the world in pursuit of all the evils that had poured out. It spread into the darkest corners of despair and destruction and wherever its faint glow glanced the oppressed felt their spirits rise and the flame of life burn more steadily.

It touched Prometheus bound hand and foot on the mountainside so he felt his marvellous creation, Mankind, was not destroyed for ever. It even touched Zeus as he looked down on Pandora, crouched beside the empty box. Such a tiny thread of light but it would be enough to ensure Zeus did not triumph completely.

Butterflies and Swimmers

Susan Gates and Peter Sutton

Lennox had only just got into the water. But he was already thinking, 'I'm getting out in a minute.'

He'd picked the wrong time to come. There were no kids here. The pool was full of serious swimmers. They had dark goggles on. They wore tight, white swimming hats. It made their heads look like giant mushrooms.

'Hey, watch out!' spluttered Lennox. 'You nearly drowned me!'

He'd got in somebody's way. So they'd just swum over him! They hadn't even noticed him. Lennox watched the person swim off, their arms going like windmills.

He did the doggy-paddle to the side of the pool.

He clung there, coughing up water, blinking his stinging eyes.

When he opened them he saw something amazing. It was beside the pool on the cold, white tiles.

'It's a butterfly!' he said, out loud.

He couldn't believe it. He peered at it, astonished.

'Hey, what are you doing here?' Lennox asked. 'In a swimming pool? How'd you get into this building? You don't belong in here!'

'You should be out there!' Lennox told the butterfly. 'Where there's trees and flowers!'

He pointed upwards. There were windows high up in the roof. You could see blue sky through them. But those windows weren't ever opened. The butterfly was trapped.

It wasn't a gorgeous, rare butterfly. Not the kind that makes you go, 'Wow! Look at that!' It was just some little white and brown thing.

Lennox shrugged and left it. He started splashing around. But all the time he kept thinking about that butterfly. So he swam back to look at it.

It was still there on the wet, slippy tiles. Lennox didn't know what to do. He looked round to see if the swimmers had seen it. But they didn't stop. They just carried on swimming. Up and down, up and down, making the pool into waves, like the sea.

Lennox wished he hadn't seen it either. He didn't want to get out of the pool to chase after it. He was a shy kid. All the serious swimmers would stare at him.

'Oh no,' he thought, squirming with horror at the thought of it. 'I'm sorry, butterfly. I can't get out! I just can't!'

The butterfly didn't move. Had it been moving before? Lennox couldn't remember.

'Well it's dead,' he decided. 'It's probably dead now.'

He was a bit sorry but mostly he felt relieved. It felt like a big responsibility had been lifted off his shoulders. It was OK. He didn't have to worry about the butterfly any more.

He doggy-paddled about a bit. He forgot all about the butterfly. But when he splashed back to the side he found he was staring straight at it.

And it was still alive.

'No, no, no!' Lennox groaned inside his head. He didn't want to look. But he had to.

It was fluttering. It was only a feeble flutter. But it definitely wasn't dead yet.

Then one of the serious swimmers did a racing turn. Slosh! Water swamped the butterfly. It was struggling.

'Oh no!' said Lennox. 'Fly away! Fly away!' He didn't want to have to look at it any more. He didn't want to think about it. He was angry with the butterfly for making him so upset.

18

'Go on, fly away! What did you have to come in here for! You stupid butterfly!'

It couldn't fly away. It was in real trouble now. Its wings were soaking wet. It toppled over, into a puddle of water. But Lennox couldn't pretend it was dead. He could see that its antennae were still quivering.

His face twisted up. It looked as he was in agony. But he was trying to think what to do. He didn't want everyone staring at him, thinking, 'What's that crazy kid doing?' It made him hot and bothered just thinking about it. But he couldn't do nothing. He couldn't just swim away.

He said, 'Hey you seen that butterfly?' to a goggled mushroom-head. But the mushroom-head swam away. It hadn't heard him.

So it was up to him. There was no one else. Suddenly he felt terribly little and lonely.

But he gave a big sigh. Then climbed out the pool.

He knelt down on the cold tiles and, very, very gently, picked the butterfly out of the puddle.

'Oh no!'

It slipped off his hand! It was falling into the water! 'I've killed it now!' thought Lennox.

He scooped at it frantically.

'Got it!'

He cupped his hands round it. Was he too late? The butterfly wasn't moving at all. Not even a tiny flicker.

19

It was all soggy. He shouldn't have waited so long! He should have climbed out sooner!

Then his worried face broke into a huge grin. He could feel wings tickling his fingers. He could definitely feel them!

It was OK. It was still alive.

Still grinning, he pattered down the side of the pool, with the butterfly safe inside his hands. He needn't have worried. The serious swimmers didn't notice him. Only a lifeguard saw him. 'Don't run!' he warned him.

Lennox dived nto the changing rooms. His problems weren't over yet. 'What am I going to do now?' he thought.

He couldn't go out into the street in his wet baggy trunks. No way! It was Saturday. It was busy out there! There would be ladies shopping. Somebody from his school might see him!

But he had to let the butterfly go outside, where it belonged. He gulped once, twice. Then he made a deperate dash for the door.

Some shoppers did see him. They saw a little kid, dripping wet, in big baggy trunks, race out of the swimming pool. They saw him lift up his hands high. Then open them flat, like a book.

They probably heard him say, 'Go on, fly away! Why don't you fly?'

The traffic roared past. The butterfly trembled on Lennox's palm. He was shivering now, from the cold. But he didn't look around him. Not at the staring shoppers. Or the traffic. All he saw was that butterfly.

'Please, fly away!'

It fluttered into the air. Lennox didn't wait to see where it went. He just ducked his head down and rushed back inside, through the changing rooms and dived into the water, splosh!

'Phew!' he gasped, coming up in a cloud of bubbles. 'Did I really do that? Out in the street? In front of all those people!' He could hardly believe it.

The serious swimmers were climbing out now. There were big, clear blue spaces in the water. Some kids were coming in.

'Think I'll stay in a bit longer,' Lennox thought.

Something made him look up through the glass roof.

And there was the butterfly, on its way to find flowers, drifting over the swimming pool on the breeze.

'See you!' said Lennox, raising his hand in a last salute.

Then he set off on his way, doggy-paddling down the pool.

The Paradise Carpet

JAMILA GAVIN ◆ KIM MARSLAND

'One knot blue, two knots yellow, three knots red, four knots green ...' The young boys chanted the pattern of the carpet they were weaving. Bony little fingers deftly drew the card down the thread; warp and weft ... warp and weft ... top to bottom, right to left ... warp and weft and knot.

Behind a loom inside a dark mud hut, crouching like caged animals, sat a line of boys. With backs against a wall, their thin arms rose and fell as they drew the threads from top to bottom, right to left, warp and weft and knot. They could have been musicians plucking at strings, but these were carpet weavers whose harmonies were of the eye not the ear as, bit by bit, the glorious patterns and hues of a rich carpet emerged in the darkness. 'One knot blue, two knots yellow, three knots red, four knots green ...' The boys

wove their thread, prompted and guided by old Rama, the only man among them, who had the pattern pinned to an upright in front of him.

'Ishwar, you're dreaming again!' bellowed a harsh voice. THWACK! The hand of the overseer struck a boy round the head.

The boy, Ishwar, faltered and nearly fell over sideways, but Bharat, crouching next to him, braced his body and managed to keep his friend upright.

'Keep your mind on the job. There'll be no supper for any of you tonight until you've woven another ten inches,' threatened the man. His great shape filled the doorway and blotted out their only source of light. Then he was gone. There was a low groan from the boys. Another ten inches before they would eat! That could take two hours or more, for this was the

most complicated carpet they had ever woven — and the whole thing was to be completed within seven months — when an ordinary carpet took at least twelve.

A wealthy man had come along the rough track to the village in his white Mercedes. When he reached the brick house of Anoup, the carpet manufacturer, he got out like a raja, surrounded by shy jostling children and deferential elders, all of whom noted the gold rings embedded in his chubby fingers, and the chunky foreign watch just glinting beneath the cuffs of his smart suit.

'I want a carpet for my daughter's dowry,' he declared. 'She is to be married next December.' (Everyone did an instant calculation. That was only seven months away.) 'And this is the pattern I want you to weave.'

Anoup took the piece of paper the rich man held out for him. He stared at it long and silently, then gloomily and apologetically shook his head. 'Impossible,' he said. 'I need at least twelve months to do an average carpet – but this ... this ... and in SEVEN months, you say ... No. Impossible.'

The rich man pulled out a fat briefcase from the car. He opened it up. There was a gasp from the onlookers. No one had ever seen so much money. Great wads of it, all stapled and bound straight from the bank. 'This is what you get now – and the rest when its finished. I'm sure you can do it. Just work a little harder – and a little longer each day, eh?' He tweaked the ear of the nearest little boy.

'I ... er ...' Anoup hesitated.

'Take it, take it ...' voices around him urged.

Anoup's brain spun. Common sense said, don't do it ... you can't do it ... But the money ... 'I'll do it. Your carpet will be ready on time.'

Anoup gave old Rama the pattern. 'You'd better study this,' he said.

Now Rama knew why Anoup had hesitated. The pattern was of a paradise garden; of strutting peacocks with sweeping tails, gold spotted deer leaping through undergrowth, squirrels coiling round tree-trunks and monkeys swinging from bough to bough; all sorts of exotic birds swooped and trilled and pecked at luscious fruit and flowers. Most extraordinary of all, was the Tree of Life, from its spreading roots at the base, rising up and up through twisting coiling branches, all the way to the top where the rays of rising sun pierced golden shafts through the leaves. It would need threads of every colour in the rainbow. 'There aren't enough hours in the day ...' Rama protested softly.

'Then we will use the hours of the night too,' Anoup retorted harshly.

Ishwar stared at the bright blue square in the doorway – the blue of the sky outside. He longed to leap up and charge into the daylight and play, play, play. He had almost forgotten what the outside was like. It was two years since his mother had brought him to this village to be bonded to

Anoup, for debts incurred in his grandfather's lifetime. Since then he had worked behind a loom in the dark, airless mud hut. It was like that for all of them; bonded and enslaved – even old Rama – and Ishwar knew he too would die in bondage, that the debt would never be paid off in his lifetime either.

Ishwar could hear the voices of the village children being taught under the neem tree to chorus out their times tables and their alphabet. Ishwar tried to listen and learn – but it was no use. He must chant for ever with the other carpet weavers, the colours of the thread they were weaving ... one knot yellow, two knots blue, three knots red, four knots green ...

The paradise garden shimmered on the loom. If he couldn't play outside, then he must roam within its green shade and splash in the stream and chase the deer and climb branch by branch up and up the Tree of Life until he reached the blue sky there on the loom. With a strange eagerness, he took up the thread and moved his card top to bottom, right to left, warp and weft and knot, as if he would weave himself into the carpet.

Exactly when the seven months were over, the white Mercedes came. The villagers watched anxiously as the rich man came before, right up to Anoup's door.

'Is it ready?'

'It is,' answered Anoup, eyeing the bulging briefcase on the back seat.

'Show it to me. You realise that if it is not exactly what I ordered, I will not take it.'

'Sir, it is exactly what you asked for in every detail,' boasted Anoup.

'I'll be the judge of that,' snorted the rich man. 'Bring it out in the daylight where I can examine it properly.'

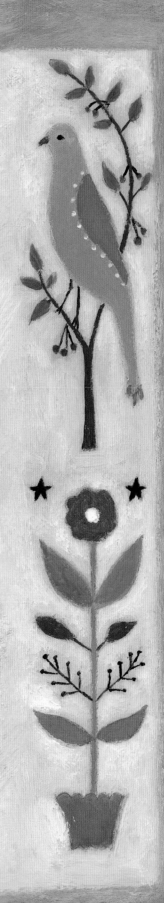

Anoup clicked his fingers. Rama and three boys ran to the hut.

'Hey, Ishwar!' exclaimed Rama, 'Wake up, boy! Help us with the carpet.'

Ishwar was sitting in his usual place behind the loom, his head leaning against the upright. He didn't respond.

'Hurry up!' bellowed Anoup impatiently. Rama and the boys lugged the carpet outside and with almost holy reverence, unrolled it. Even the villagers gasped in amazement at the beauty and workmanship. It was a miracle. They beamed with pride.

The rich man came forward till his nose nearly touched the pile. Inch by inch he scrutinised the carpet. Suddenly, he roared with fury. 'What's this!' he shouted. 'I didn't ask for this! What kind of idiotic thing have you done here! I can't take it – not with THIS!' He dragged the carpet out of their hands and trampled it into the dust. Then leaving the villagers appalled and stunned, the rich business man got into his car and sped off at top speed.

Nobody moved. Fearful eyes turned to Anoup. He was standing as if turned to stone. At last he clicked his fingers. In horrified silence they held out the carpet. Anoup's expert eye began at the top and scanned the carpet, as he had done twenty times each day. In his mind's eye, he wove each thread himself. He panned along the twisting branches of the Tree of Life, the glowing colours of humming birds and nightingales, dropping down through ten shades of green leaves and a dozen shades of blossoms of red, pink, purple and violet; he noted the golden fur of a deer darting through the grass, the hundred eyes of a peacock's tail shimmering near a silver fountain ... and ...?

Then Anoup's body shuddered. He shuddered so hard, they heard his teeth rattle, and the bones of his fingers clicking as he ground his knuckles into his fist.

'What is it?' murmured the villagers. 'What has he seen?' They surged forward. Speechless with rage, Anoup pointed to a spot deep in the undergrowth. Almost hidden among blossom and foliage, the young face of a boy peered up at the Tree of Life, an arm upstretched, ready to climb.

'Ishwar!' Rama muttered under his breath. 'It's Ishwar!'

'Ishwar!' The name was shrieked in vengeance! The villagers rushed to the hut.

The boy still leaned against the loom as if resting his aching head. Anoup strode over and kicked him. The boy slipped forward, face down, on to the earth floor. When they rolled him over, they saw he was dead.

Daddy's Coming Home Today

Beverley
Naidoo
and
Daniel
Pudles

'Daddy's coming home today!'
my little sister cartwheels
heels over head
springs beside me
and laughs.
'Don't count chickens before
  they hatch,'
I growl.
She lets my words drop on the
  floor.

'Daddy's coming home today!'
my little sister spins
yellow daisies whirling
on her sky-blue skirt
and claps her hands.
'You don't fill your belly
  painting pictures of bread,'
I glower.
Chestnut eyes wide
she watches my words sputter
  and fizzle.

'Daddy's coming home today
and Mama's going to make
  chicken!'
my little sister clicks
fingers like castanets
swinging hair bobbing
and stamps her feet.
'Mama!'
I yell.
'Tell her not to ...'

Mama comes to the doorway.
Little sister leaps
a baby kangaroo
seeking her pouch.
'Daddy's coming home today!'
she sings softly
rocking in Mama's arms.
'Tell her not to Mama!'
I plead.
'Tell her!'

Mama's eyes touch me
'We all need dreams, son,'
she says gently.

I turn my face away.

My dreams fight with
  nightmares

Drowning in darkness
I cling to a rope
alone in the shadows
of a wall
that grows
taller
with each glance
Palms sweating
I heave myself upwards
centimetre by centimetre
swinging and bobbing
like a cork
spinning until my head
cartwheels
and my fists grasp
slippery cold bars
Superhuman
I squeeze
through iron
into the thick night
of a mist-filled cell

Keys click
metal clangs
My heart judders
Then
close by
I hear breathing
steady and sure
and a quiet voice
reaches me
'Come here, son!'

I stretch up my fingers
and touch the prickles
of my father's beard
I feel strong limbs
draw me up
enclose me
'We all need dreams, son.'
I hold him tight
and fight my tears

When I open my eyes
I am wrapped in Mama's
  arms.
Little sister plants
a kiss on my cheek
and skips away.

'Daddy's coming home
  tomorrow!'
she chants.

DARE TO BE DIFFERENT

Malorie Blackman and Jane Ray

'Why can't I?'

'Because you can't. No one can. It's not allowed,' Mum argued.

'But why? Mum, I need to ...'

'I said no,' Mum exploded. 'Aca, forget about it. It's never been done.'

'But nothing would ever get done in this world if everyone used the excuse that it hadn't been done before to stop them. We wouldn't have the wheel or the microwave or cars or TVs or ...'

'Aca, have your ears stopped working suddenly? I said and I meant – NO. How many times are we going to have

this conversation?'

'But Mum ...'

'I don't want to hear it.' Mum waved her hands dismissively. 'And I hope for your sake you haven't discussed this ... this nonsense with anyone else.'

'It's not nonsense,' I mumbled.

Why was it that every time I had this conversation with Mum and Dad, it always ended the same way? They could hear me, but they never listened.

'Aca, this is dangerous nonsense which could get all of us into serious trouble. You are never, ever to talk

about this again. D'you understand me?'

'I'm not going to stop thinking about it just because you tell me not to talk about it.'

'DO YOU UNDERSTAND ME?'

'Yes, Mum.'

Mum didn't wait to hear any more. She marched off. I ran upstairs to my bedroom, slamming the door as hard as I could behind me.

'I've got to do this and ... and I'm going to,' I muttered as I lay on my bed. 'I don't care what Mum and Dad say.'

But that was a lie. Because I did care what they said. Of course I cared. If I went through with this, they'd be so hurt. And everyone would know. I'd be different. Different meant isolation and loneliness and being stared at and pointed to. Different required courage. I had a choice of course. I could stifle what I felt inside until my true feelings, my true self withered away and died. I knew plenty of other people, even some in my own family, must have done exactly that. But I couldn't.

My mind was made up. For better or

33

worse I was going to go for it! The way I saw it, if I couldn't be true to myself, how could I be true to anyone else? The following day, I taped a letter to the mirror in Mum and Dad's bedroom.

Dear Mum and Dad,

I'm sorry but I have to do this. Please don't worry about me. I'm going to be fine. I'm only going away for my sixteenth birthday. Just long enough to do this my way. I'll be back after three days. Please don't try to find me. I don't want you to stop me. Please understand. I love you. See you soon.

All my love,
Aca.

They wouldn't understand of course. How could they? Why should they? I was about to bring shame and disgrace raining down on them. Maybe one day they would understand enough to forgive me.

I used the little money I had with me to rent myself a first floor room in a seedy dive where I knew I wouldn't be disturbed even if the building was on fire. I admit I was scared, more scared than I'd anticipated, but there was a strange cocktail of exhilaration racing through my body as well. I was really going to do it. I took off my clothes and laid down on the bed, wondering what I should do first. And then it occurred to me. All I had to do was accept the part of me that everyone else denied

existed. Just accept it. That was all. I fell asleep, with my arms wrapped around myself, and never before had I known such peace.

When I awoke, I felt exactly the same. Well, not exactly. I felt unwashed and gungy, but I didn't feel different. How long had I been asleep? It was hard to tell. My room was in darkness. The only light came from one small patch on the wall which reflected the yellow street light outside. I checked my watch. It was after midnight. How many days had passed? I turned on my small pocket telly and tried to find a news channel. When I finally heard the date, it was a shock. I'd been asleep for the whole three days. I hadn't expected that. So why didn't I feel any different? Had nothing happened? Hadn't it worked?

I went into the shower cubicle in the corner of the room to wash the sleep off my body. I tried not to think about the disappointment raging through me or what I should do next. Go home with my tail between my legs and take my punishment?

Then, without warning, my back began to hurt. Well, my shoulder blades to be precise. A dull, scratching ache at first, which was more off than on, but it grew persistently worse, until I was clawing at my back in agony. It wasn't an ache any more. My back was on fire. It felt like my shoulder blades were being ripped out of my body. I cried out with the pain, but there was no one around to hear me and certainly no one around to care.

And just when I thought I'd pass out from the pain in my back, it suddenly stopped. Just like that. I stayed in the shower for several minutes afterwards, until the water ran chilly then icy cold.

Only then did I step out.

Once I was out of the shower, I dug into my still packed bag and took out clean pants and a T-shirt, wondering what had just happened. Maybe I'd slept in a funny position and that was my back protesting? I pulled the T-shirt over my head, only I had real trouble getting it past my shoulders. Each time I tried, it hurt. I went over to the cracked mirror in the corner of the room to see what was the problem.

And that was when I saw them for the first time. My wings. Beautiful golden wings still folded against my body. I let out a shriek of delight. I don't know what I'd been expecting but this wasn't it. On our sixteenth birthday, each member of my race was given a special drug to keep them awake for three days and nights. Three days and nights which constituted the 'Time of Change'. It'd been that way for centuries. Everyone was terrified of the Time of Change. It was strictly forbidden to sleep during that time because that was the one and only time in our lives when the 'monster' within could be unleashed. But I'd slept through mine and there was no monster – just beautiful golden wings. I had to try them. Now. At once. I ran out of my room and threw myself down the stairs to get to the road. The moment the midnight breeze whispered across my back, I clenched my shoulders and my wings unfurled. And then before I knew it, I was up and up and up. Flying, flapping away from the world below me. I could fly. I was different. No doubt there would be many who would shun me. But surely once everyone saw that I hadn't become a monster, I wouldn't be the only one with wings for long. Look at me! I could fly. Yes, I was different, but so what?! If being different meant flying – even flying all alone – then it was worth it.

Now we are Free

ELANA BREGIN AND NIKI DALY

'Tell us a story, Grandpa,' begged Nomsa.

'Yes, tell us the one about the days in the old South Africa, when you were growing up,' said Albert.

'You have heard that story a hundred times,' said Grandpa. 'I am tired of telling it to you.'

He was in a cross mood today because his back was hurting him.

'Susannah hasn't heard it,' Lettie said, pulling her friend forward. 'Tell it to us one more time. Please, Grandpa?'

Grandpa sighed and put aside his newspaper.

'When I was young, life in South Africa was not like it is today. People were separated by their colour.'

'Black ones, white ones, brown ones, yellow ones,' interrupted Albert.

'And purple and green ones!' shouted Sipho, who was too young to understand much.

'Who is telling this story,' said

38

Grandpa crossly, 'you or me?'

He waited until they were quiet again. 'Life was very hard for black people in those days. They were forced to live in horrible places called Homelands, far away from everyone else. There was no work there and no food. So mothers and fathers had to leave their children and travel far away to look for jobs.'

'How stupid!' said Susannah, 'Why was it like that?'

'That was the law.'

'It was a stupid law!'

Grandpa nodded his head. 'It was called Apartheid. And it made a lot of people very unhappy.'

'But there's no Apartheid any more,' said Lettie. 'Now we are free to live wherever we want to.'

'I know where I want to live,' Sipho said. 'Inside the forest, in a big tree!'

'I'll go stay with dolphins under the sea,' laughed Nomsa.

'My house will be on a mountain-top, high in the air,' said Susannah.

'I'll be like the wind and live every-where!' Albert said.

'Sssh,' said Lettie. 'Let Grandpa tell his story. Go on, Grandpa.'

'Yes, Grandpa, tell us about how school was in your day,' Albert said.

'Ah, school,' said Grandpa, getting his pipe out. 'Yes, there was Apartheid there too. If you were a white child,

then all your schooling was free and you got the best of everything. But if you were black, it was not easy to get a good education. Our schools were very poor. And we were forced to learn different things from the other children. The law said that the only jobs black people could get were as labourers and servants. So we were not allowed to learn things that would make us too clever.'

'I wouldn't like that!' said Albert. 'I don't want to be a labourer or a servant. I want to be a scientist and know all there is to know.'

'We're going to be engineers and build bridges for show,' said Lettie and Susannah, joining hands into a high arch.

'I want to be an astronaut and fly off to the moon,' said Nomsa, doing a little twirl.

'I'm going to be the Weatherman in the weather balloon!' shouted Sipho, jumping up to touch the sky.

'Aaai, you children!' Grandpa said. 'I wish you'd stop shouting and dancing around me like that. You're making my head hurt as well as my back.'

But he couldn't help smiling at their

antics. He watched Lettie and Susannah giggling as they patted their hands together.

'You two are very lucky you did not live in old South Africa,' he told them. 'It would not have been so easy for you to be friends then. In those days, it was forbidden for children of different colours to go to the same places. Or visit each other's homes. Or play in the parks together, or even ride on the same buses.'

'How terrible!' cried Lettie and Susannah, hugging each other.

'The old South Africa sounds like a very awful place,' Nomsa said. 'I'm very glad we did not have to grow up in it.'

'It sounds like a horrible zoo,' agreed Susannah, 'with all the people locked in cages.'

'But now the cages are open,' Albert laughed, grabbing Sipho and tickling him, 'and we are free children.'

'Yes my noisy birds, you are free children,' smiled Grandpa, giving each of them a hug. 'Why don't you spread your wings now and fly away for a little while? And give your old grandpa some peace!'

FREEDOM

BY LANGSTON HUGHES

FREEDOM WILL NOT COME
TODAY, THIS YEAR
    NOR EVER
THROUGH COMPROMISE OR FEAR.

•

I HAVE AS MUCH RIGHT
AS THE OTHER FELLOW HAS
    TO STAND
ON MY OWN TWO FEET
AND OWN THE LAND.

•

I TIRE SO OF HEARING PEOPLE SAY,
Let things take their course.
Tomorrow is another day.
I DO NOT NEED MY FREEDOM WHEN I'M DEAD.
I CAN NOT LIVE ON TOMORROW'S BREAD.
    FREEDOM
    IS A STRONG SEED
    PLANTED
    IN A GREAT NEED.
    I LIVE HERE, TOO
    I WANT FREEDOM
    JUST AS YOU.

SARA FANELLI

The Happy Prince

Oscar Wilde and Bee Willey

High above the city, on a tall column, stood the statue of the Happy Prince. He was gilded all over with thin leaves of fine gold, for eyes he had two bright sapphires, and a large red ruby glowed on his sword-hilt.

He was very much admired indeed. 'He is as beautiful as a weathercock,' remarked one of the Town Councillors who wished to gain a reputation for having artistic tastes; 'only not quite so useful,' he added, fearing lest people should think him unpractical, which he really was not.

'Why can't you be like the Happy Prince?' asked a sensible mother of her little boy who was crying for the moon. 'The Happy Prince never dreams of crying for anything.'

'I am glad there is someone in the world who is quite happy,' muttered a disappointed man as he gazed at the wonderful statue.

'He looks just like an angel,' said the Charity Children as they came out of the cathedral in their bright scarlet coats and their clean white pinafores.

'How do you know?' said the Mathematical Master. 'You have never seen one.'

'Ah! but we have, in our dreams,' answered the children; and the Mathematical Master frowned and looked very severe, for he did not approve of children dreaming.

One night there flew over the city a little swallow. His friends had gone away to Egypt for six weeks before, but he had stayed behind, for he was in love with the most beautiful Reed. He had met her early in the spring as he was flying down the river after a big yellow moth, and had been so attracted by her slender waist that he had stopped to talk to her.

'Shall I love you?' said the Swallow, who liked to come to the point at once, and the Reed made him a low bow. So he flew round and round her, touching the water with his wings, and making silver ripples. This was his courtship, and it lasted all through the summer.

'It is a ridiculous attachment,' twittered the other Swallows; 'she has no money, and far too many relations'; and indeed the river was quite full of Reeds. Then, when the autumn came they all flew away.

After they had gone he felt lonely, and began to tire of his lady-love. 'She has no conversation,' he said, 'and I am afraid that she is a coquette, for she is always flirting with the wind.' And certainly, whenever the wind blew, the Reed made the most graceful curtsies. 'I admit that she is domestic,' he continued, 'but I love travelling, and my wife, consequently, should love travelling also.'

'Will you come away with me?' he said finally to her, but the Reed shook her head, she was so attached to her home.

'You have been trifling with me,' he cried. 'I am off to the Pyramids. Good-bye!' and he flew away.

All day long he flew, and at night-time he arrived at the city.

'Where shall I put up?' he said; 'I hope the town has made preparations.'

Then he saw the statue on the tall column.

'I will put up there,' he cried; 'it is a fine position, with plenty of fresh air.' So he alighted just between the feet of the Happy Prince.

'I have a golden bedroom,' he said softly to himself as he looked round, and he prepared to go to sleep; but just as he was putting his head under his

wing a large drop of water fell on him. 'What a curious thing!' he cried; 'there is not a single cloud in the sky, the stars are quite clear and bright, and yet it is raining. The climate in the north of Europe is really dreadful. The Reed used to like the rain, but that was merely her selfishness.'

Then another drop fell.

'What is the use of a statue if it cannot keep the rain off?' he said; 'I must look for a good chimney-pot,' and he determined to fly away.

But before he had opened his wings, a third drop fell, and he looked up, and saw – Ah! what did he see?

The eyes of the Happy Prince were filled with tears, and tears were running down his golden cheeks. His face was so beautiful in the moonlight that the little Swallow was filled with pity.

'Who are you?' he said.

'I am the Happy Prince.'

'Why are you weeping then?' asked the Swallow; 'you have quite drenched me.'

'When I was alive and had a human heart,' answered the statue, 'I did not know what tears were, for I lived in the Palace of Sans-Souci, where sorrow is not allowed to enter. In the day-time I played with my companions in the garden, and in the evening I led the dance in the Great Hall. Round the garden ran a very lofty wall, but I never cared to ask what lay beyond it, everything about me was so beautiful. My courtiers called me the Happy Prince, and happy indeed I was, if pleasure be happiness. So I lived, and so I died. And now that I am dead they have set me up here so high that I can see all the ugliness and all the misery of my city, and though my heart is made of lead yet I cannot choose but weep.'

'What! is he not solid gold?' said the Swallow to himself. He was too polite to make any personal remarks out loud.

'Far away,' continued the statue in a low musical voice, 'far away in a little street there is a poor house. One of the windows is open, and through it I can see a woman seated at a table. Her face is thin and worn, and she has coarse, red hands, all pricked by the needle, for she is a seamstress. She is embroidering passion-flowers on a satin gown for the loveliest of the Queen's maids-of-honour to wear at the next Court ball. In a bed in the corner of the room her little boy is lying ill. He has a fever, and is asking for oranges. His mother has nothing to give him but river water, so he is crying. Swallow, Swallow, little Swallow, will you not bring her the ruby out of my sword-hilt? My feet are fastened to his pedestal and I cannot move.'

'I am waited for in Egypt,' said the Swallow. 'My friends are flying up and down the Nile, and talking to the large lotus-flowers. Soon they will go to sleep in the tomb of the great King. The King is there himself in his painted coffin. He is wrapped in yellow linen and embalmed with spices. Round his neck is a chain of pale green jade, and his hands are like withered leaves.'

'Swallow, Swallow, little Swallow,' said the Prince, 'will you not stay with me for one night, and be my messenger? The boy is so thirsty, and the mother so sad.'

'I don't think I like boys,' answered the Swallow. 'Last summer, when I was staying on the river, there were two rude boys, the miller's sons, who were always throwing stones at me. They never hit me, of course; we swallows fly too well for that, and besides I come of a family famous for its agility; but, it was a mark of disrespect.'

But the Happy Prince looked so sad that the little Swallow was sorry. 'It is very cold here,' he said; 'but I will stay with you for one night, and be your messenger.'

'Thank you, little Swallow,' said the Prince.

So the Swallow picked out the great ruby from the Prince's sword, and flew away with it in his beak over the roofs of the town.

He passed by the cathedral tower, where the white marble angels were sculptured. He passed by the palace and heard the sound of dancing. A beautiful girl came out on the balcony with her lover. 'How wonderful the stars are,' he said to her, 'and how wonderful is the power of love!'

'I hope my dress will be ready in time for the State ball,' she answered; 'I have ordered passion-flowers to be embroidered on it; but the seamstresses are so lazy.'

He passed over the river, and saw the lanterns hanging to the masts of the ships. He passed over the Ghetto, and saw the old Jews bargaining with each other, and weighing out money in copper scales. At last he came to the poor house and looked in. The boy was tossing feverishly on his bed, and the mother had fallen asleep she was so tired. In he hopped, and laid the great ruby on the table beside the woman's thimble. Then he flew gently round the bed, fanning the boy's forehead with his wings. 'How cool I feel!' said the boy, 'I must be getting better'; and he sank into a delicious slumber.

Then the Swallow flew back to the Happy Prince, and told him what he had done. 'It is curious,' he remarked, 'but I feel quite warm now, although it is so cold.'

'That is because you have done a good action,' said the Prince. And the little Swallow began to think, and then he fell asleep. Thinking always made him sleepy.

When day broke he flew down to the river and had a bath. 'What a remarkable phenomenon!' said the Professor of Ornithology as he was passing over the bridge. 'A swallow in winter!' And he wrote a long letter about it to the local newspaper. Everyone quoted it, it was full of so many words that they could not understand.

'Tonight I go to Egypt', said the Swallow, and he was in high spirits at the prospect. He visited all the public monuments, and sat a long time on the top of the church steeple. Wherever he went the Sparrows chirruped, and said to each other, 'What a distinguished stranger!' so he enjoyed himself very much.

When the moon rose he flew back to the Happy Prince. 'Have you any commissions for Egypt?' he cried; 'I am just starting.'

'Swallow, Swallow, little Swallow,' said the Prince, 'will you not stay with me one night longer?'

'I am waited for in Egypt,' answered the Swallow. 'Tomorrow my friends will fly up to the Second Cataract. The river-horse couches there among the bulrushes, and on a great granite throne sits the God Memnon. All night long he watches the stars, and when the morning star shines he utters one cry of joy, and then he is silent. At noon the yellow lions come down to the water's edge to drink. They have eyes like green beryls, and their roar is louder than the roar of the cataract.'

'Swallow, Swallow, little Swallow,' said the Prince, 'far away across the city I see a young man in a garret. He is leaning over a desk covered with papers, and in a tumbler by his side there is a bunch of withered violets. His hair is brown and crisp, and his lips are red as a pomegranate, and he has large and dreamy eyes. He is trying to finish a play for the Director of the Theatre, but he is too cold to write any more. There is no fire in the grate, and hunger has made him faint.'

'I will wait with you one night longer,' said the Swallow, who really had a good heart. 'Shall I take him another ruby?'

'Alas! I have no ruby now,' said the Prince; 'my eyes are all that I have left. They are made of rare sapphires, which were brought out of India a thousand years ago. Pluck out one of them and take it to him. He will sell it to the jeweller, and buy firewood, and finish his play.'

'Dear Prince,' said the Swallow, 'I cannot do that;' and he began to weep.

'Swallow, Swallow, little Swallow,' said the Prince, 'do as I command you.'

So the Swallow plucked out the Prince's eye, and flew away to the student's garret. It was easy enough to get in, as there was a hole in the roof. Through this he darted, and came into the room. The young man had his head buried in his hands, so he did not hear the flutter of the bird's wings, and when he looked up he found the beautiful sapphire lying on the withered violets.

'I am beginning to be appreciated,' he cried; 'this is from some great admirer. Now I can finish my play,' and

he looked quite happy.

The next day the Swallow flew down to the harbour. He sat on the mast of a large vessel and watched the sailors hauling big chests out of the hold with ropes. 'Heave a-hoy!' they shouted as each chest came up.

'I am going to Egypt!' cried the Swallow, but nobody minded, and when the moon rose he flew back to the Happy Prince.

'I am come to bid you good-bye,' he cried.

'Swallow, Swallow, little Swallow,' said the Prince, 'will you not stay with me one night longer?'

'It is winter,' answered the Swallow, 'and the chill snow will soon be here. In Egypt the sun is warm on the green palm-trees, and the crocodiles lie in the mud and look lazily about them. My companions are building a nest in the Temple of Baalbek, and the pink and white doves are watching them, and cooing to each other. Dear Prince, I must leave you, but I will never forget you, and next spring I will bring you back two beautiful jewels in place of those you have given away. The ruby shall be redder than a red rose, and the sapphire shall be as blue as the great sea.'

'In the square below,' said the Happy Prince, 'there stands a little match-girl. She has let her matches fall in the gutter, and they are all spoiled. Her father will beat her if she does not bring home some money, and she is crying. She has no shoes or stockings, and her little head is bare. Pluck out my other eye, and give it to her, and her father will not beat her.'

'I will stay with you one night longer,' said the Swallow, 'but I cannot pluck out your eye. You would be quite blind then.'

'Swallow, Swallow, little Swallow,' said the Prince, 'do as I command you.'

So he plucked out the Prince's other eye, and darted down with it. He swooped past the match-girl, and slipped the jewel into the palm of her hand. 'What a lovely bit of glass!' cried the little girl; and she ran home, laughing.

Then the Swallow came back to the Prince. 'You are blind now,' he said, 'so I will stay with you always.'

'No, little Swallow,' said the poor Prince, 'you must go away to Egypt.'

'I will stay with you always,' said the Swallow, and he slept at the

Prince's feet.

All the next day he sat on the Prince's shoulder, and told him stories of what he had seen in strange lands. He told him of the red ibises, who stand in long rows on the banks of the Nile, and catch goldfish in their beaks; of the Sphinx, who is as old as the world itself, and lives in the desert, and knows everything; of the merchants, who walk slowly by the side of their camels and carry amber beads in their hands; of the King of the Mountains of the Moon, who is as black as ebony, and worships a large crystal; of the great green snake that sleeps in a palm tree, and has twenty priests to feed it with honey-cakes; and of the pygmies who sail over a big lake on large flat leaves, and are always at war with the butterflies.

'Dear little Swallow,' said the Prince, 'you tell me of marvellous things, but more marvellous than anything is the suffering of men and of women. There is no Mystery so great as Misery. Fly over my city, little Swallow, and tell me what you see there.'

So the Swallow flew over the great city, and saw the rich making merry in their beautiful houses, while beggars were sitting at the gates. He flew into dark lanes, and saw the white faces of starving children looking out listlessly at the black streets. Under the archway of a bridge two little boys were lying in one another's arms to try and keep themselves warm. 'How hungry we are!' they said. 'You must not lie here,' shouted the watchman, and they wandered out into the rain.

Then he flew back and told the Prince what he had seen.

'I am covered with fine gold,' said the Prince, 'you must take it off, leaf by leaf, and give it to my poor; the living always think that gold can make them happy.'

Leaf after leaf of the fine gold the Swallow picked off, till the Happy Prince looked quite dull and grey. Leaf after leaf of the fine gold he brought to the poor, and the children's faces grew rosier, and they laughed and played games in the street. 'We have bread now!' they cried.

Then the snow came, and after the snow came the frost. The streets looked as if they were made of silver, they were so bright and glistening; long icicles like crystal daggers hung down from the eaves of the houses, everybody went about in furs, and the little boys wore scarlet caps and skated on the ice.

The poor little Swallow grew colder and colder, but he would not leave the Prince, he loved him too well. He picked up crumbs outside the baker's door when the baker was not looking, and tried to keep himself warm by flapping his wings.

But at last he knew that he was going to die. He had just enough strength to fly up to the Prince's shoulder once more. 'Good-bye, dear Prince!' he murmured, 'will you let me kiss your hand?'

'I am glad that you are going to Egypt at last, little Swallow,' said the Prince, 'you have stayed too long here; but you must kiss me on the lips, for I love you.'

'It is not to Egypt that I am going,' said the Swallow. 'I am going to the House of Death. Death is the brother of Sleep, is he not?'

And he kissed the Happy Prince on the lips, and fell down dead at his feet.

At that moment a curious crack sounded inside the statue, as if something had broken. The fact is that the leaden heart had snapped right in two. It certainly was a dreadfully hard frost.

Early the next morning the Mayor was walking in the square below in company with the Town Councillors. As they passed the column he looked up at the statue: 'Dear me! how shabby the Happy Prince looks!' he said.

'How shabby, indeed!' cried the Town Councillors, who always agreed with the Mayor; and they went up to look at it.

'The ruby has fallen out of his sword, his eyes are gone, and he is golden no longer,' said the Mayor; 'in fact, he is little better than a beggar!'

'And there is actually a dead bird at his feet!' continued the Mayor. 'We must really issue a proclamation that birds are not to be allowed to die here.' And the Town Clerk made a note of the suggestion.

So they pulled down the statue of the Happy Prince. 'As he is no longer beautiful he is no longer useful,' said the Art Professor at the University.

Then they melted the statue in a furnace, and the Mayor held a meeting of the Corporation to decide what was to be done with the metal. 'We must have another statue, of course,' he said, 'and it shall be a statue of myself.'

'Of myself,' said each of the Town Councillors, and they quarrelled. When I last heard of them they were quarrelling still.

'What a strange thing!' said the overseer of the workmen at the foundry. 'This broken lead heart will not melt in the furnace. We must throw it away.' So they threw it on a dust-heap where the dead Swallow was also lying.

'Bring me the two most precious things in the city,' said God to one of His Angels; and the Angel brought Him the leaden heart and the

dead bird.

'You have rightly chosen,' said God, 'for in my garden of Paradise this little bird shall sing for everyone, and in my city of gold the Happy Prince shall praise me.'

The Gulf

GERALDINE MCCAUGHREAN AND ROSEMARY WOODS

The cold, thin air in the back of his throat was like swallowing swords, but he ran until sweat burst through his skin, until the sweat dried to salt. He ran until every searchlight, floodlight and white-winking barrack window was out of sight and he was running in utter darkness. He ran until night gave way to morning, and every moment he expected to hear shouts or motors or the barking of dogs on his trail.

With sunrise he allowed his hopes to rise too, like a hot, orange ball of flame within his chest. Might he after all make good his escape? Might he reach safety, against all the odds? No one ever did, they had told him. No one ever would. But the hope kept rising in his throat until it buckled his mouth into a smile.

Then he reached the gulf.

He almost ran straight into it – a gorge of such dizzying depth that the river in the bottom was only a green thread; a canyon so wide that a horse at full gallop could not have leapt even halfway across. And its sides were sheer.

Juan fell to his knees, grazing his forehead on the bark of a dead, fallen tree, his arms over his head. Had he come this far to meet disappointment like a snake across his path? There was no way over. The gulf stretched as far as the eye could see to right and left. He could leap into it or wait at the brink of his pursuers to catch up with him. But he was done for. It was true. No one ever escaped. No one ever would.

When he raised his head, Juan saw a little girl watching him. She stood on the far side of the canyon, rubbing a twist of grass between her hands. 'Want to cross over?' she said. In the silence of the empty landscape her voice floated easily over to him. She did not have to shout.

She spoke the dialect of the neighbouring country. The river gorge must be the border, then. Juan had reached the border – a stone's throw from safety. 'Is there a bridge? Anywhere? A bridge?' he called.

'No. No bridge ... But I could fetch my sisters.' She put her fingers in her mouth and whistled shrilly. Juan gave a laugh somewhere between a bark and a sob. Much good her sisters would do him.

The girls came dawdling out from the long grass and regarded him with the same solemn brown eyes. Each was rubbing a twist of grass between her hands.

'He wants to cross over,' said the sister.

'Better tell the brothers,' they said.

Ten boys emerged from the swashing grass, carrying sickles and armfuls of grass. They sat

down on the far side of the ravine, dangling their legs over the rim. Their hands began to work in that same nervous, habitual motion, rubbing the grass stems together into long tasselled cords.

'Go home,' said Juan, glancing over his shoulder. He did not want them to witness either his tears or his recapture. He had no idea how much of a lead he had gained on his pursuers. Eight hours? Nine?

'They chasing you?' called one of the boys, swatting flies.

'I thought I could reach the border. But the gulf … I didn't know …'

Their sunburned faces expressed no sympathy, no sadness at his predicament. Their small brown hands just went on twisting grass.

'I'll tell the mothers,' said the littlest boy, and ran off, his bare feet unsettling flies in clouds.

The village must have been just over the ridge, for he soon returned, towing his mother by the hand. For the first time, Juan realised that the grass-twirling was not a nervous habit but a livelihood. The mothers – handsome women with shining plaits to which their babies clung – were also twirling the grass together into fibres, their big hands worn horny by the coarse stems. They contemplated Juan with large, dark-fringed eyes. 'You need help,' said one.

Juan laughed hollowly. 'I am past helping. This gulf did for me.'

The women called the children together, took their cords of grass, and began, simply by rubbing, to splice the thin lengths into thicker, longer ones. 'Fetch the grandmas and grandpas,' they told the littlest boy.

Away he went, and fetched back with him the old people of the village — mumbling, bent, bone-weary old bodies

who shook their heads and clutched their shawls round them, even though the day was hot. One old matriarch, her hat as big as a bundle of laundry, flumped down amid her skirts, and the women laid their grass-cords at her feet, as if paying homage. Her whispering palms twirled their individual cords into one long rope, with a deftness which defied belief. For a few blessed minutes Juan watched with such intent fascination that he forgot his own peril and strained to make out what magical process, what cunning craftmanship could twist grass into rope.

Then, with a jolt of hope sharp as a kick, he realised that the rope was for him – to get him over the ravine.

What well-meaning, simple fools! Inwardly he raged with bitter laughter. Even if they succeeded in making a cable strong enough to carry the weight of a man, long enough to span the gulf, how would they get the end across to him? Impossible! So much work and for what? Around him the evening breeze sprang up, and Juan found he had sat all day by the gulf watching the children and grandparents and mothers opposite labour over the rope, which now lay coiled at the old woman's feet.

That same breeze carried on it the sound of jeep engines, of sirens, of his pursuers.

'What's the point? What's the point?' he bawled, and his voice dropped into the ravine like a rock fall.

The little girl – the one he had seen first – lifted up a coil of the immense rope to show him. It was all she could do to raise it off the ground. 'Father will help,' she said. 'He is coming soon.'

It reduced him to tears – this little mite's touching, ridiculous trust in her father. What would he prove to be, after all, but yet another pigeon-chested peasant in a straw hat, chewing betel nuts and hoping for a quiet life. A man like Juan.

The little girl's father proved, however, to be a big, energetic man – a hunter. When he arrived, his jeans and shirt dusty after a day on the plateau, he found the village assembled by the ravine, saw Juan, saw the rope, and instantly re-strung his bow. His grandmother threaded a needle with sewing thread, and stuck it through the grass rope, then gave the thread to her grandson. He tied it to his arrow and, without a word to Juan … fired it straight at him.

The arrow gouged up the soil between Juan's feet. With trembling fingers, he snatched the cotton, winding the loops so tight round his hand that his fingers went blue. The rope was heavy, but the sewing thread did not break. Like a great anaconda, the rope's end sagged its way across the ravine, and Juan made it fast around the log. The strongest of the villagers took hold of the other end and braced themselves.

The jeeps were visible now, bouncing over the rough terrain, the evening sun flashing on their windscreens. In the normal way of things, Juan could never have brought himself to do what he did next. But after so many people had done so much, he could hardly hesitate. Hanging like a tree sloth under the grass rope he crabbed his way over the yawning, heart-numbing terror of the vertiginous drop, fixing all his thoughts on the beauty of the hawser, the thousand different shades of yellow and green all interwoven into one speckled cable. How could something so strong be made of such frail component parts? The seed-dust made him sneeze.

The jeeps skidded to a halt just as hands – old and young and callused – closed in Juan's hair and round his arms and through his belt and pulled him to safety. Then the villagers dropped their end of the great rope into the ravine. It thumped against the far wall, shedding a shower of seeds.

Juan jumped to his feet and shook a defiant fist at the men on the opposite bank. In his raised hand was a single twist of grass.

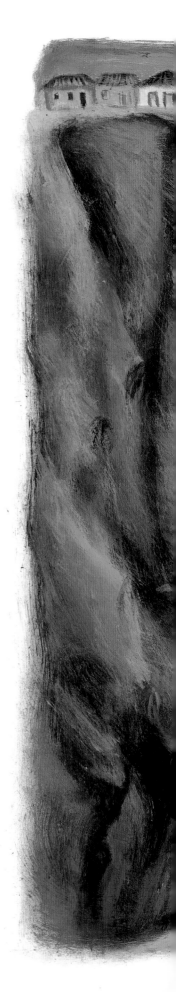

Daniel and the Lions

DAVID ARMITAGE

1 It pleased Darius to set over the kingdom an hundred and twenty princes, which should be over the whole kingdom;

2 And over these three presidents; of whom Daniel *was* first: that the princes might give accounts unto them, and the king should have no damage.

3 Then this Daniel was preferred above the presidents and princes, because an excellent spirit *was* in him; and the king thought to set him over the whole realm.

4 Then the presidents and princes sought to find occasion against Daniel concerning the kingdom; but they could find none occasion nor fault; forasmuch as he *was* faithful, neither was there any error or fault found in him.

5 Then said these men, We shall not find any occasion against this Daniel, except we find *it* against him concerning the law of his God.

6 Then these presidents and princes assembled together to the king, and said thus unto him, King Darius, live for ever.

7 All the presidents of the kingdom, the governors, and the princes, the counsellers, and the captains, have consulted together to establish a royal statute, and to make a firm decree, that whosoever shall ask a petition of any God or 8

8 Now, O king, establish the decree, and sign the writing, that it be not changed, according to the law of the Medes and Persians, which altereth not.

9 Wherefore king Darius signed the writing and the decree.

10 Now when Daniel knew that the writing was signed, he went into his house; and his windows being open in his chamber toward Jerusalem, he kneeled upon his knees three times a day, and prayed, and gave thanks before his God, as he did aforetime.

11 Then these men assembled, and found Daniel praying and making supplication before his God.

12 Then they came near, and spake before the king concerning the king's decree; Hast thou not signed a decree, that every man shall ask *a petition* of any God or man within thirty days, save of thee, O king, shall be cast into the den of lions? The king answered and said, The thing *is* true, according to the law of the Medes and Persians, which altereth not.

13 Then answered they and said, before the king, That Daniel, which *is* of the children of the captivity of Judah, regardeth not thee, O king, nor the decree that thou hast signed, but maketh his petition three times a day.

14 Then the king, when he heard *these* words, was sore displeased with himself, and set *his* heart on Daniel to deliver him: and he laboured till the going down of the sun to deliver him.

15 Then these men assembled unto the king, and said unto the king, Know, O king, that the law of the Medes and Persians *is*, That no decree nor statute which the king establisheth may be changed.

16 Then the king commanded, and they brought Daniel, and cast *him*

into the den of lions. *Now* the king spake and said unto Daniel, Thy God whom thou servest continually, he will deliver thee.

17 And a stone was brought, and laid upon the mouth of the den; and the king sealed it with his own signet, and with the signet of his lords; that the purpose might not be changed concerning Daniel.

18 Then the king went to his palace, and passed the night fasting: neither were instruments of musick brought before him: and his sleep went from him.

19 Then the king arose very early in the morning, and went in haste unto the den of lions.

20 And when he came to the den, he cried with a lamentable voice unto Daniel: *and* the king spake and said to Daniel, O Daniel, servant of the living God, is thy God, whom thou servest continually, able to deliver thee from the lions?

21 Then said Daniel unto the king, O king, live for ever.

22 My God hath sent his angel, and hath shut the lions' mouths, that they have not hurt me: forasmuch as before him innocency was found in me; and also before thee, O king, have I done no hurt.

23 Then was the king exceeding glad for him, and commanded that they should take Daniel up out of the den. So Daniel was taken up out of the den, and no manner of hurt was found upon him, because he believed in his God.

24 And the king commanded, and they brought those men which had accused Daniel, and they cast *them* into the den of lions, them, their children, and their wives; and the lions had the mastery of them, and brake all their bones in pieces or ever they came at the bottom of the den.

25 Then king Darius wrote unto all people, nations, and languages, that dwell in all the earth; Peace be multiplied unto you.

26 I make a decree, That in every dominion of my kingdom men tremble and fear before the God of Daniel: for he *is* the living God, and stedfast for ever, and his kingdom *that* which shall not be destroyed, and his dominion *shall be even* unto the end.

27 He delivereth and rescueth, and he worketh signs and wonders in heaven and in earth, who hath delivered Daniel from the power of the lions.

28 So this Daniel prospered in the reign of Darius, and in the reign of Cyrus the Persian.

Only a
Stone

Bernard Ashley and Colin Backhouse

They were ball mad, Carl and Luke – football, volleyball, basketball. The most anyone ever heard of them was the bounce of a ball on concrete and yells of 'Yeah!' as points and baskets were scored and goals went in. The back garden at number 128 Bardon Street, was the Olympic Arena.

Being younger, Luke had to be goalie or back four in games of football. Carl was striker and radio commentator. 'This young lad is sheer genius!' (himself); 'And another lucky save!' (Luke).

But Olympic arenas have a decent height to them, they have grandstands and executive boxes – and it's rare for balls to go over into the street. Whereas the stadium at 128 had just a wooden fence round it, with a wire extension over the top at one end, put up by their neighbours at the back. That was the end where the basket was, and the goal. This was where most shots went, where the high misses were mostly saved by the wire mesh. But it was different down the sides. A bad bounce or an unlucky header and over went the ball –

out of the stadium. But not for long, as a rule. Old Mrs Moore at number 126 remembered having children, so she always threw balls back, and the Taylors at number 130 still had children, so they never

their garden to be all paving and tiles and statues, with a fountain. Every evening until the light went they were out there sweeping the slabs, raking the gravel, or sitting on scrapey metal chairs to drink coffee.

Of course, it had to happen. One evening in a game of football, Carl chested down a throw-out from Luke, took it on his right knee, hoisted it for a volley, but caught it awkwardly on the side of his foot. 'And even this young striker can make the odd mistake ...' Over went the ball to number 126. There was a sudden silence – except for the trickling of the fountain.

Carl faced the fence, knew the Safars were out there. He was ready with 'Cheers!' on his lips to say thank you for throwing it back. But the ball didn't come back. All he could hear was the scrape of a chair and that trickle, trickle, trickle ...

Luke called him something and after a snarling match the pair of them huffed indoors. Frustrated, Carl took a kick at a stone which dared to be in his path. And the stone followed the football over the

minded, either.

It was when Mrs Moore went to Sheltered Accomodation that ball matters changed. Mr and Mrs Safar moved in, who came from Iraq – and they were keen for fence and cracked into the fountain of number 126. Trickle, trickle, splash!

Oh, no! Carl knew he'd hear more than the scrape of a chair about this. And he'd hardly got halfway up the stairs to his bedroom when the front doorbell rang.

Mum answered it before Carl could get started on any advance excuses.

It was Mrs Safar with a plastic bag. She smiled politely and was invited in. Carl crept down the stairs and had to go in when he and Luke were summoned.

'This ball,' said Mrs Safar, sitting on the settee at Mum's invitation, looking younger in the black hyjab round her head now she was up close. 'We're not against playing ball. Far from it. Our sons loved all those games, we always miss the sounds, I hear them in my dreams ...'

'Grown up?' asked Mum.

Mrs Safar nodded. 'And didn't get out of Iraq.'

There was one of those moments while the boys looked at their mother and thought their own thoughts about someone loved who wasn't around any more. Their dad.

'We're going to grow a vine, on something up high, so we don't have to worry about unlucky bouncing, but ...'

Carl swallowed. He knew there'd be a 'but' coming; he knew about the stone. Now Mrs Safar brought it from the plastic bag and laid it flat on her hand. A smooth pebble.

'This is different, isn't it? It doesn't bounce, it would go through a vine. It could have hurt someone.'

Mum looked at Carl and Carl studied the carpet. Intently, Mrs Safar held out the stone to give it back to him.

'S'all right, it's only a stone.' Carl tried to sound sorry and humble.

'Only a stone?' Mrs Safar's hand suddenly clamped the stone tight, then she slowly opened her fingers, like revealing a small creature which might fly away. 'Only a stone?'

Mum hadn't blinked. Carl and Luke were staring at Mrs Safar.

'This stone is as old as the earth, it will still be here when we've been gone for millions of years, when people no longer walk this planet, when there's not a book or a city in existence ...'

'I s'pose you're right.' Mum looked as if she might be about to take the stone and put it on top of the telly like a Madonna or a Buddha.

Mrs Safar got up. She put the stone in Carl's hand. 'Stones and man, man and stones, one and always the other ...'

'David and Goliath!' said Luke.

'And the Flintstones,' said Carl.

'Weapons, tools, statues; beautiful art and terrible acts; stone and rock stand for

the best and the worst of us ...' Mrs Safar
was getting up.

'The worst?' asked Carl. 'It was only an
accident ...'

He wished he'd kept quiet. Mrs Safar
sat down again. 'They stone people to
death in some parts of the world – and
always someone ready to throw the first
stone.'

'Wouldn't be me,' said Luke.

'So no ball games till we build the high
fence?'

The boys nodded.

'No football, no stones?'

They kept on nodding; and Mrs Safar
went.

'Out of the way with these,' Mum said.
She gave Carl the ball and the stone.

He threw the ball to Luke, but kept the
stone sitting on his hand.

'And what are you going to do with
that?' Mum asked.

'Dunno,' he said. 'Think I might keep it.'
And he put it in his pocket. One thing was
for sure – it was never going to be only a
stone, not this one.

People Equal

James Berry

Christopher Corr

Some people shoot up tall.
Some hardly leave the ground at all
Yet people equal. Equal.

One voice is a non-sugar tomato
Another is sweet mango.
Yet people equal. Equal.

Some people rush to the front.
Other people feel they can't.
Yet people equal. Equal.

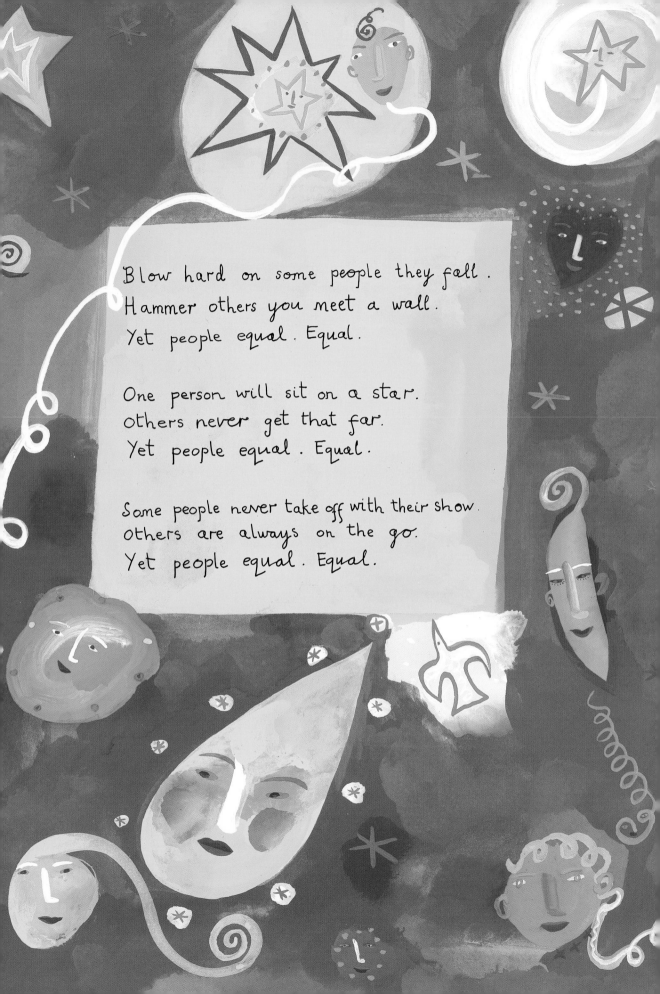

Blow hard on some people they fall.
Hammer others you meet a wall.
Yet people equal. Equal.

One person will sit on a star.
Others never get that far.
Yet people equal. Equal.

Some people never take off with their show.
Others are always on the go.
Yet people equal. Equal.

Beauty and the Beast

Henrietta Branford and Quentin Blake

There was once a young woman who was so beautiful that she had no other name but Beauty. She lived with her father and her two greedy sisters. Beauty's father was both rich and kind and his three children had everything they wanted – until one sad, bad day their father lost all his money.

'I'm ruined,' he said. 'I must ride to town and sell whatever I can. If I get enough money I'll bring you each a present.'

'Goody,' said one greedy sister. 'I want a ruby ring!'

'I want a diamond tiara, a real one!' said the other greedy sister.

'I'd like a red rose please,' said Beauty.

'Is that all, Beauty?' asked her father.

'Of course not,' said Beauty. 'I want you to come safe home.'

'So I shall, my darling,' said her father. And off he rode on Hoggin his horse, clip clop.

The three girls waited anxiously for his return – Beauty because she loved him and her sisters because of the presents. He did not get enough money in town to buy presents and he couldn't find a red rose anywhere. 'Oh well,' he said. 'It can't be helped. Home, Hoggin.' And off they went.

Now, Hoggin could find his way home with his eyes shut and so could his master – usually. But not this time. This time was different. Snow fell; it made the road look different. Even the trees looked strange – tall, dark and ghostly. By and by the sun went down and the woods filled up with shadows. Hoggin and his master were well and truly lost.

Something rustled overhead and Hoggin shied. 'It's just the wind in the leaves, Hoggin old boy,' said Beauty's father. All the same, he couldn't stop thinking about robbers hiding behind the tree-trunks. Hoggin couldn't stop thinking about wolves. Both of them shook with fear but they went bravely on. What else could they do?

By and by, bright lights shone through the darkness. 'Go that way, Hoggin,' said his master. 'Make for the lights.' Hoggin did.

There, half hidden by a thick high wall, stood an old stone palace with pointed towers. Steps led down into a garden. Iron gates swung open. In went Hoggin and his master and the gates clanged shut behind them, almost trapping Hoggin's tail.

Hoggin clattered up to the great palace door. High above, arched windows looked down emptily. A curtain blew out in the wind. Beauty's father knocked and knocked again but nobody came to the door. Presently he led Hoggin round to the stables, where straw lay deep and oats filled the manger. 'Goodnight, Hoggin my friend,' he said. 'Sleep tight.'

He left Hoggin champing his oats and went back to the palace door and this time it creaked open all by itself. Beauty's father stood still on the doorstep. A cold wind blew at his back; indoors, a warm fire glowed. He shivered one shiver and in he went. Wouldn't you have done the same?

Inside the palace he found food on

the table and clean dry clothes laid out by the fire to warm. Should he, could he, help himself? Would it be right? You must remember that he was cold and wet and hungry. And the food smelled good. Very good. Pretty soon he had changed his clothes and eaten his supper. He sat by the fire warming his knees and in no time he nodded off to sleep.

When he woke up the next morning he was determined to find whoever lived in the palace and say thank you. He searched the place from attic to cellar and back again. There was nobody at home. Next he searched the garden; still he found no one. But he did find a velvety red rose that smelled of summer in the frosty garden. 'Perfect for Beauty,' he said to himself. And he picked it.

The very second that the rose stem

snapped, a roar shook the garden. Beauty's father whipped around and there, right behind him, stood a great gruff beast with curling horns and yellow eyes and tusks like a boar and claws like garden rakes. 'How dare you steal my rose?' bellowed the beast. 'You'll die for that!' Beauty's father fell to his knees.

'Please,' he begged, 'don't kill me. My children need me. I picked the rose for Beauty, my youngest. I would have asked you if I could have found you!'

'Harrumph!' huffed the beast; steam gushed from his red throat. 'Bring me Beauty and I will let you live. But she must come of her own free will or not at all. And if she won't come, you must come back here and prepare to die!'

Beauty's father gulped and nodded and ran to the stable for Hoggin. He galloped all the way home, crying out loud at the thought of his Beauty living with the Beast. When he got home he told his three daughters all that had happened.

'What, no presents?' scoffed the two greedy sisters. But Beauty kissed her father and smiled. 'Don't cry,' she said. 'I'll go, and willingly, to save your life.'

She packed a few belongings and climbed up behind her father on Hoggin's strong back. Sadly they rode back to the palace in the wood. Sadly, they kissed goodbye.

All that day Beauty wandered through the palace. With every door she opened she wondered if the beast was waiting on the other side. But he wasn't. Beauty explored the garden too but found no sign of the Beast. It was evening and she was eating her supper when she heard the sound of his breath behind her chair and smelt the hairy beary smell of him. 'Good evening, Beauty. May I sit with you while you

eat?' he asked in his growly, prowly voice.

'Of course you may,' said Beauty, trying not to show how scared she was.

Each day Beauty spent alone in the palace. She examined every room and most of them were full of interesting things, but she was often bored and lonely. Each evening the beast came to sit with her. 'He's terribly ugly,' thought Beauty. 'But I don't think he's wicked. If he was going to hurt me, he would have done it by now.' Slowly she grew less frightened of him. You might even she

began to grow fond of him. He certainly grew fond of her.

One evening he looked at her in a special way. His yellow eyes smiled softly and his long tusks shone in the candlelight. His hairy face blushed red as roses. 'Beauty,' he asked, in his growly prowly voice, 'will you marry me?'

'Oh, no, no, no!' gasped Beauty, and she ran from the room.

After that the Beast asked every night, his yellow eyes shining with love, 'Beauty will you marry me?'

And each time Beauty answered: 'No, no, no!'

'I know that you're not happy,' said the Beast one night after supper. 'Tell me what would make you happy, Beauty?'

'I want to go home and see my father again,' said Beauty. 'I miss him so much.'

'Then you shall go,' said the Beast. 'Take this magic ring. Turn it round on your finger when you are ready to come back to me. But Beauty – don't stay away too long or I shall die of missing you.'

Beauty had a happy time at home, working in the garden with her father, cooking his favourite meals, showing him how much she still loved him. But her greedy sisters were jealous and wished her gone. 'Go back to your ugly

beast,' they teased. 'You belong with him now!'

Beauty was surprised to find how much she missed the Beast. She thought about him often but still she stayed on with her father. She put off going back for as long as she could. Then one night she dreamed that she was lying in bed in the palace. Moonlight was shining through the window. She ran downstairs and out into the garden. She walked until she came to a path where a rose grew tangling up an apple tree. There lay the Beast, quite still, with his face in the grass.

Beauty woke up and found her own face wet with tears. She said goodbye to her grumpy sisters, kissed her father and turned the magic ring on her finger.

This time she really was back in her palace bedroom. Down she ran and out into the garden, calling 'Beast! Beast! Where are you? I've come home!'

She searched and searched, palace and garden, but she dared not, dared not look under the rose until at last it was the only place left to look. Slowly, she tiptoed down the grassy path.

There on the ground lay the Beast. His horns were broken, his claws were blunt from digging in the earth, his eyes were swollen up with tears. Only then did Beauty understand how much she loved him. 'Darling Beast,' she whispered, stroking his bristly hair, 'I love you, I do. I'd marry you too, if you still wanted me. Only now it's too late. I'm sorry, so sorry that I stayed away so long.'

Beauty lay down beside the Beast and cried bitter tears. Sadness makes you tired. Soon Beauty fell asleep. When she woke up, her Beast was gone. 'Beast, darling Beast! Where are you?' Beauty cried.

'I'm here,' said a voice behind her.

Beauty looked round. There on the path stood a beautiful young prince. 'I was a prisoner until you loved me,' he said. 'Now, at last, I'm free.'

'It isn't you I want,' wailed Beauty. 'It's my darling beast. I stayed away too long and now he's dead and gone and it's my fault, all my cruel fault!'

'Look at me, Beauty,' said the prince. 'Can't you see who I am?'

Then Beauty looked, and Beauty saw.

And they were happy ever after.

ACKNOWLEDGEMENTS

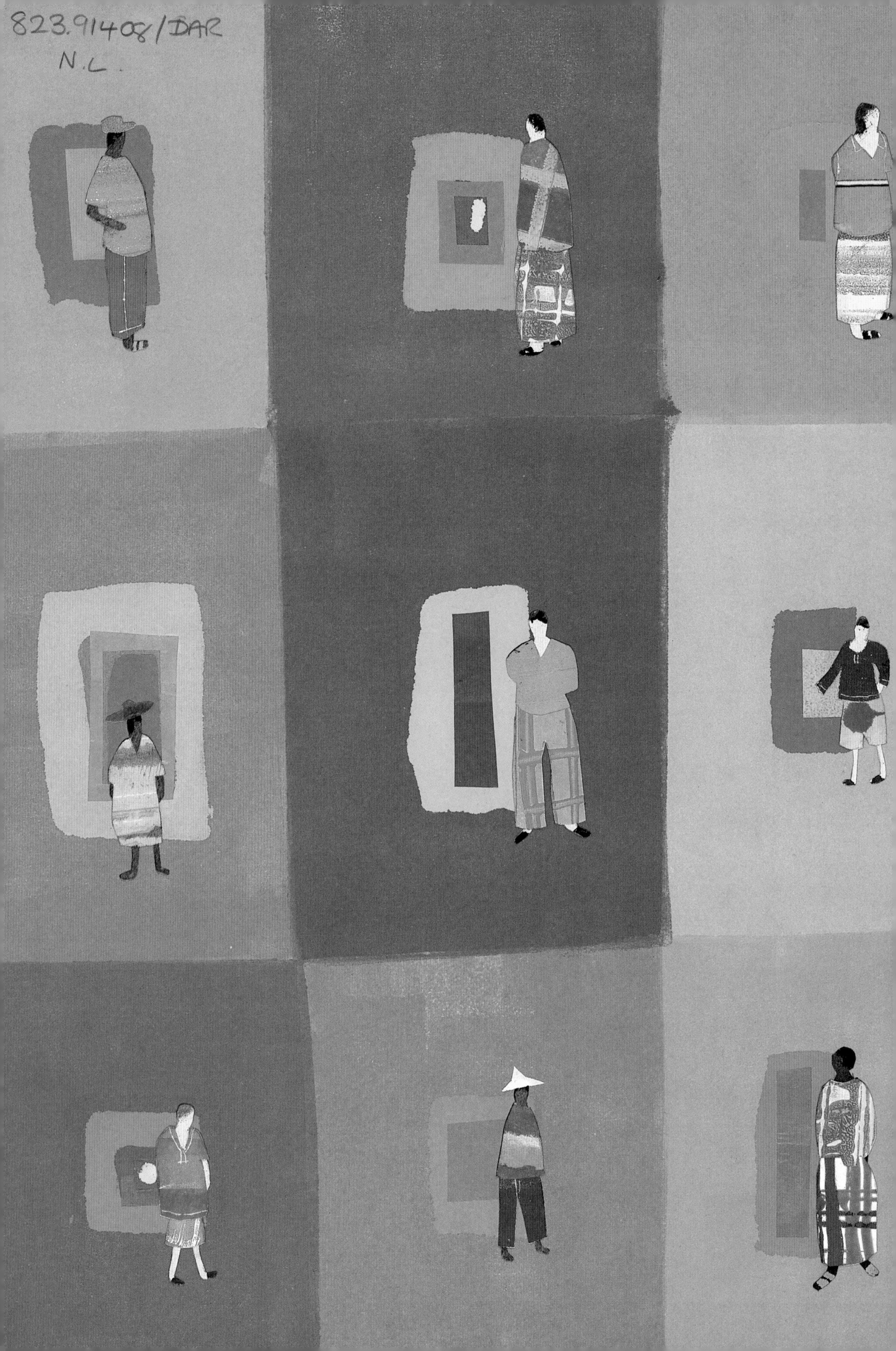